MW01075708

THE MAGIC DOOR
Francine Paino

ISBN: 978-1-7326489-2-0

ACKNOWLEDGMENTS

MANY THANKS TO JUSTINE, KP, KATHY,
AND HELEN FOR THEIR PATIENCE AND INPUT.

ILLUSTRATIONS THROUGH CANVA. THANK YOU
CALLIOPE, LEXEY, AND MADDIE, FOR YOUR ARTISTIC
CONTRIBUTIONS.

AS ALWAYS, I SEND LOVE AND GRATITUDE TO ALL OF MY
TREASURES OF INSPIRATION!

YOU KNOW WHO YOU ARE.

CHAPTER 1
HOW IT ALL STARTED

Trapped!

It was pouring rain. Mom, Dad, and Grandfather were off on a golf outing, and I was stuck at Grandma's house with my ten-year-old sister Callista, and my two girly cousins, Lynda, eight, and Mary seven. On the floor, playing and fighting over trains were my two boy cousins, Daniel five, and Tomas three. The third, six-month-old Joseph Robert, we called him JR, was snoring in his carrier.

I'm Andrew, the oldest, and the one Grandma expected to help with the little ones. But being stuck at Grandma's was usually fun. She always had great games, and when the weather was good, she loved to play catch with us.

Sometimes, we took long walks, up and down the hills around her street. We'd make up stories about the animals that lived in the greenbelts there. She always said, "Imagining is an important part of learning."

We could ask Grandma anything. She had great answers—most of the time. But when we'd ask how old she was, she'd smile, and wink from behind her really big, black-framed glasses and say, "I'm old enough to be your grandmother."

Today, though, was not so fun. Something strange was happening, and we were trapped inside because the weather was awful. The sky got darker, and the feeling was weird.

I'd been ready to tear my hair out since the first crack of thunder and bolt of lightning sent us skittering in the house.

Outside, mighty thunder rolled across the sky and rattled the walls and windows. We could hear tree branches whipping and cracking against the house, while lightning bolts flashed in the windows.

Inside, there was a different kind of storm.

Grandma turned on all the lights and tried to get us interested in other things. "How about a nice game of Name that Country?" She held up a huge map of the world. We all shook our heads: No.

"Maybe Hangman to practice your spelling," she suggested.

"Nah," we all chorused.

"Mary, play the piano. We can have a sing-along."

"Nope," was the answer to that.

"Let's make pizza," my sister Callista said, clapping her hands. We all loved to make pizza with grandma.

“We will soon, but the dough hasn't risen yet." She explained that on rainy days, pizza dough could take longer to be ready. "Why don't you all play cards while we wait?"

Lynda and Mary decided to play Go Fish at the kitchen table while Grandma stood at the stove, making the pizza sauce. The game didn't last long.

"Grandma, she's cheating," cried Lynda, her gold curls popping out from her head every which way.

"I'm not. You're just a sore loser," shouted Mary. Her long blond ponytail whipped from side to side as she shook her head.

Lynda stuck her tongue out at Mary; Mary threw her Go Fish cards at Lynda.

Callista lay on the couch, her long black hair fanned out like a peacock's tail behind her. Her permanently affixed headphones covered her ears;

her black eyes were focused on the fantasy book she was reading. She paid no attention to the fracas going on. Her body language said, Don't bother me!

She's no help, I thought.

“Hey, gimme that," yelled 5-year-old blond-haired Daniel, whose long locks fell into his eyes. Lord, the boy needed a haircut. He grabbed the caboose out of brown-haired, buzz-cut, 3-year-old Tomas's hand.

Tomas screamed, "No. It's mine."

Grandma turned on the TV. "Watch Mickey Mouse and calm down," she said. But they didn't. When Grandma wasn't looking, Tomas took a swing at Daniel; Daniel tackled Tomas in retaliation. I jumped in the middle to separate them. Tomas swung again; Daniel ducked, and I ended up with a punch in my left eye. It took all my self-control not to use my Tai Kwon Do, black-belt skills on both of them.

"That's it!" Grandma shouted. "Time out. Every one of you to your corners."

What a mess. We'd never heard Grandma give that order while waving her wooden spoon in the air. We all jumped and did as she said, even me!

"But I didn't do anything!" Callista lamented, holding her hands over her heart in her most melodramatic pose.

"Doesn't matter," Grandma said. "To your corner."

While grandma dealt with Callista, I shoved a quantum physics book under my shirt and hoped I'd at least get some reading done.

Now, with only a chorus of snivels and sobs, we could hear the wind blowing hard, and rain hitting the windows like pellets.

W-A-A-N-N-K-K! A horn blared from the TV.

"Yow," cried Tomas. He jumped up from his corner behind the kitchen table and grabbed Grandma's leg.

"Holy Cow," I yelled.

Callista heard it even with her headphones on. "What was that, Grandma?" she shouted.

"Oh gosh, that's a tornado warning," Lynda said. "Are we going to blow away?"

"No, my darlings, we won't blow away." Using her obey me immediately tone, she ordered, "Quick now, take the pillows and cushions from the couch and follow me." She lifted JR's carrier, and one by one, we followed Grandma through her bedroom, across her bathroom, and into her ginormous walk-in closet that had only one set of double doors and no windows.

We looked around. We'd all been in the closet before but were never allowed to play in there. It was big with lots of clothing rods holding grandma's dresses above a long chest of drawers.

Grandfather's pants and jackets hung on rods on the opposite wall, with two shoe racks beneath them. There was a big open space in the middle.

"Stay here until the all-clear sounds." Grandma handed me a big flashlight. "Just in case the lights go out," she said.

"I don't want to stay here. I want to stay with you," Tomas said, giving Grandma his most dazzling smile.

It didn't work.

Grandma patted his buzz-cut head. "My closet is a very fun place. There are lots of interesting things in it."

"What could be interesting in a clothes closet?" I asked.

"After the storm passes, you'll tell me. Just one rule. Do not open the top drawer in the long chest under my dresses. Those things cannot be played with."

"What things?" asked Mary.

"Things that cannot be played with," Grandma answered and handed Lynda a bottle of milk. "If JR wakes up, give him the bottle." Grandma turned to me. "Test the flashlight, Andrew."

I did. "It works," I said.

Grandma turned to Callista. "No headphones. You and your brother are the oldest, and you must take care of your younger cousins."

Callista frowned. Her lower lip stuck out at the start of her famous pout.

"No, sulking," Grandma said. Callista handed over her headphones.

We all stood there, hugging our cushions. I thought the others looked scared. I'm sure I did too.

"You're safe in here, and it will be over before you know it," said Grandma. She was smiling kind-a funny.

"Where are you going?" I asked.

She rumpled my thick, sandy hair. "I'm going to watch the weather," she answered and walked out of the closet, closing the doors behind her.

Outside, a low rumble built up, but before it became the next crack of thunder, I heard the doors click.

She'd locked us in!

I didn't feel too good about that, but I didn't want to upset my sister or my cousins. We stood there in the center of the closet, listening to the howling wind outside.

"Maybe we should sit on the floor," I said.

"You're not the boss," Callista snapped.

"I don't want to," cried Tomas.

"I want Grandma," shouted Mary.

Daniel reached for Lynda's hand.

"Don't grab me," said Lynda, pushing him away. Daniel went over to Tomas. They stood together and cried.

"Oh, for goodness sake," Callista said, losing patience with the boys. "Stop crying!"

Then the lights went out.

"Oh, no," Lynda cried out.

"Yikes!" yelled Mary.

"Help," Tomas sobbed.

We all reached for each other in the dark. Then I remembered, I had a flashlight.

I flicked it on. "Whew. That's better." I said.

Callista dropped her pillow to the floor. "I'm sitting down." We all dropped our cushions along with Callista and huddled together.

Whoosh, bang, thwap. The storm was getting worse. The wind was whistling; rain and branches and other things banged against the sides of the house. During a short lull in the storm, Mary jumped up. Her blond ponytail bobbed up and down. "I'm bored." She looked around and pointed to the chest under grandma's dresses. In one leap, she was in front of it and pulling the top drawer out.

Callista warned, "Grandma said not to open that drawer."

"You are going to get us in trouble," said Lynda. "Close the drawer."

Mary inched it out a little more. "I can't see. It's too dark. There's nothing in here but some wrinkled up cloth," she said and stamped her foot.

"Hmmm." I walked over to shine the flashlight into the drawer. The others joined us as Mary pulled it out a little more.

There was a faint sound, like a chirp.

"What was that?" Lynda asked.

Ch-i-r-r-r-r-p. This time louder.

Mary yanked the drawer all the way out. The chirping was shrill and louder still, under the wrinkled fabric. Then, *Neebey, Neebey, Neebey.*

The *chirping* and *Neebey-ing* pierced our hearing. We covered our ears and ducked our heads, but Mary forgot to close the drawer.

Without warning, out flew a strange creature as big as the fattest pigeon I'd ever seen. It had four legs, bright blue feathers, and one huge, glowing yellow eye in the center of its head. It flapped its two long wings, hovering above our heads, then it landed and sat onthe clothing rod above Grandma's dresses.

Chiirrrrrpppp. The strange bird stared down at us, and we stared up into its one golden eye. Then it gave one loud cry: *NEEEBEEEY*, and out flew more bird-like creatures. They were bright reds, yellows, and blues. Some were black and shiny. They all had one glowing yellow eye, two long wings, and four legs. They circled above us and stared down. *NEEBEY*, they cried, then flew up to the ceiling. I tried to follow them with the flashlight, but they were too quick.

Thunk. Thunk. Bump. Thump.

We heard the birds bumping into the ceiling. Then the clickety-click of their feet as they ran down the wall behind Grandpa's suits and jackets, chirping and shrieking like mad. Then everything stopped.

"Oh, gosh. Grandma is going to be so mad," said Lynda, pointing at her sister. "And it's all your fault."

Mary sobbed. "I didn't mean to do it. The wind made me do it."

"No," Lynda scolded, her yellow curls springing this way and that as she shook her head. "You made yourself do it."

Mary cried harder. Daniel went over and hugged Mary's leg.

I sighed. "It doesn't matter now. We gotta get them back in the drawer. But where are they?"

We looked and looked, but we couldn't see them.

“Where, oh, where could they be?” Tomas’s blue-gray eyes shone with tears.

“Probably behind the clothes,” I answered, wanting to reassure everyone, I said, “Don’t worry. We’ll get them back,” but I didn’t have a clue as to how.

“How do you call a bird?” Daniel asked.

We all thought about that and tried different sounds.

Daniel called “Caw, caw.” Nothing.

Tomas said, “Tweet, tweety-tweet. Again nothing.

Callista tried, “Chirp, chirp.”

I swung the flashlight around the closet, trying to find them.

Lynda was about to push Grandma's dresses aside when the flashlight went out.

“Oh, no. Now we can’t see anything,” Mary said. We pressed our bodies together in the dark closet.

I was getting nervous. What were we to do?

“At least JR is sleeping through it all,” whispered Lynda, making sure his carrier was securely in the middle of us.

“Look!” Callista said. She pointed to grandma's dresses.

A sliver of light shone behind them.

"What is that?" Lynda asked. She and Callista pushed the dresses aside; more light came into the closet.

"And what's that?" Mary asked, pointing to the center of the wall where the light came from. It spun, glittered, sparked and grew. We watched in amazement until it stopped and took shape.

"It's a door," Tomas cried out. "A big wooden door."

"And there's a handle," Daniel said. I stepped up and grabbed it. Pulling as hard as I could did nothing. The door didn't budge. I took a deep breath and tried again. "Uragh!" I pulled with all my might.

The door creaked open, and an ocean of light poured into the closet. The birds, hiding behind the clothes, began to chirp and screech.

Ne-e-e-bey! Ch-i-r-r-r-r-r-p! Ne-e-e-bey!

Out of the drawer flew more of these strange creatures in all the colors of a rainbow. Through the door and into the bright light, they soared.

Mary ran after them. "C' mon," she yelled. "We need to get them back."

I picked up JR's carrier. "Grab the bottle," I said. Callista stuffed the bottle in her waistband and grabbed Lynda, who grabbed Daniel's hand; Daniel took Tomas's hand.

"Hurry," Mary called from beyond the door.

Having second thoughts, I yelled, "Wait. Mary, come back," but my words were drowned by a new burst of howling wind and things banging against the house.

Was it my imagination, or was the big wooden door in the wall beginning to fade?

I grabbed Callista's hand. "Everyone, hold on to one another. Don't let go," I said and pulled them through the door in the wall behind grandma's dresses.

CHAPTER 2
A STRANGE LAND

We tumbled through the door and into the light. It was so bright we couldn't see Mary; we couldn't see anything.

"Where are you, Mary?" we called.

"Here," she said." Our eyes adjusted, and we saw her step out from behind a tree, holding the strangest looking flowers. They were bright reds, yellows, and oranges, and they looked like flower petals, but they weren't solid. They fizzed like sparklers on July 4th.

"Did you see the trees? They're gold and silver," she said. "Touch them. They're smooth, not rough like real tree bark."

We walked to the nearest gold and silver tree and ran our fingers down their smooth trunks.

"Wow," said Daniel. "They are."

"Look at the flowers," Lynda said, pointing to the oodles and oodles of flowers on the side of the dirt path. She and Callista went to the flowerbeds to pick their own fizzy flowers. They both reached for the same one.

"Hey," Lynda yelled. "I was going to pick that one."

"I got it first," Callista answered and tried to pull the flowers from Lynda's hands, but Lynda was quick. She hugged the strange flowers to her chest and turned away.

Daniel and Tomas wandered around, picking up shiny stones. At first, they tossed them gently, then they threw them harder and harder at each other.

"Ow," cried Tomas.

"C' mon guys," I said. "We're here to get the birds."

Suddenly, the ground began to shake. *Rrumbble. Thummble. Rrumbble.* The girls dropped the exotic flowers, and Tomas and Daniel dropped the stones. We grabbed on to one another. The rumbling got louder; the ground shook harder. Our teeth chattered, our knees knocked, and our arms trembled.

"I'm scared," Callista uttered, her voice trembling like the ground.

As suddenly as the rumbling had started, it stopped. But we still shook as we clung to each other and squeezed our eyes shut.

"Don't be afraid," a voice said. "You are safe here."

"Who said that?" Mary screeched.

"I did," said the voice.

Courage, I told myself even though I didn't feel too brave. I lifted my head to sneak a peek.

"Wow!" I said. "Open your eyes. Look!"

Before us, sparkling in the sunlight, was a huge, black shining elephant, glittering with gold and silver. It raised its trunk, and its ears flapped back and forth like enormous fans. Then it spoke.

"Welcome, children. My name is Elefantia, and you are now in the Gold and Silver Forest."

"We came through that door," I said, pointing behind me. Elefantia nodded her head. "I know. We have been waiting for you."

"You knew we were coming?"

"Yes, Andrew." Elefantia said then greeted everyone by name.

Mary stood up straight and thumped her fists on her hips. "How did you know we were coming?"

"Yeah," said Daniel, his blue eyes wide with wonder. He slapped his fists on his hips, imitating his sister.

"And how do you know our names?" Lynda asked.

"The Neebey birds told us."

"What's a Neebey bird?" asked Tomas.

Elefantia pointed her trunk to the tops of the gold and silver trees. We looked up. The Neebey birds perched on the branches stared down at us.

NEEBEY, they sang out.

"That means hello, in Neebey-speak," Elefantia said, waving her trunk at the birds.

"Those are the birds from Grandma's dresser," Mary said. Then she remembered why we were there. "Oh, no," she bawled. "We gotta get them back."

Elefantia raised her trunk. "Don't cry. We will help you."

"We?" I asked. Who are we?"

"Follow me," said Elefantia, turning and walking down the path. Each step she took vibrated the ground. We looked at each other, but didn't move.

“Should we?” Lynda asked. The others looked confused and scared.

I shrugged, “Maybe we better.”

“Wait a minute,” Callista held up her hand. “You can’t tell us to go.”

“Yeah,” said Daniel. “You go.”

“I wanna go back to grandma’s closet.” Tomas stamped his foot.

W-A-A-A-A! Elefantia raised her trunk high, blasted air at us, and stomped one foot. The ground under our feet shook harder.

We shut up.

“Follow me!” she ordered, then wagged her trunk and bellowed out a huffing sound that hit us like a hot wind. She marched off through the gold and silver trees, muttering, “These children fight about everything.”

Lynda looked back at where we came from and poked me. “The door isn’t there anymore,” she whispered.

“Nuts!” I said. “Well, if we can’t go back, then we’d better follow her.”

Callista murmured, “Before Elefantia blasts us again.” We followed the elephant through the gold and silver forest. We emerged from the trees at the end of the woods.

"Look out there," Elefantia said, pointing her trunk to a valley. We stood beside the elephant and stared. There wasn't a leaf on a tree, a blade of grass, or a flower on a stem.

Tomas stepped up. "Oh, it's ugly." He pointed at the dead looking land. Elefantia hung her head, and a great wash of tears ran down the sides of her trunk. We gathered close to her.

"The evil Cracklor birds steal the color from our land. If you try to stop them, they bite," she said, showing her bitten leg.

A tear ran down Mary's face. Daniel stroked the elephant's trunk.

Elefantia pulled in a long sniffle then raised her head. "I shouldn't cry. Sagezza told us that one day, children who could dream would pass through the door to help us, and here you are."

"Who is Sagezza?" Callista asked.

"She is the wisest of the three Magica sisters. Cattiva is the evil one who sends the Cracklors to steal our color, and Befana sees the good and special powers in children."

"Why is Cattiva stealing the color?" asked Lynda.

"Befana will explain. Here she comes now."

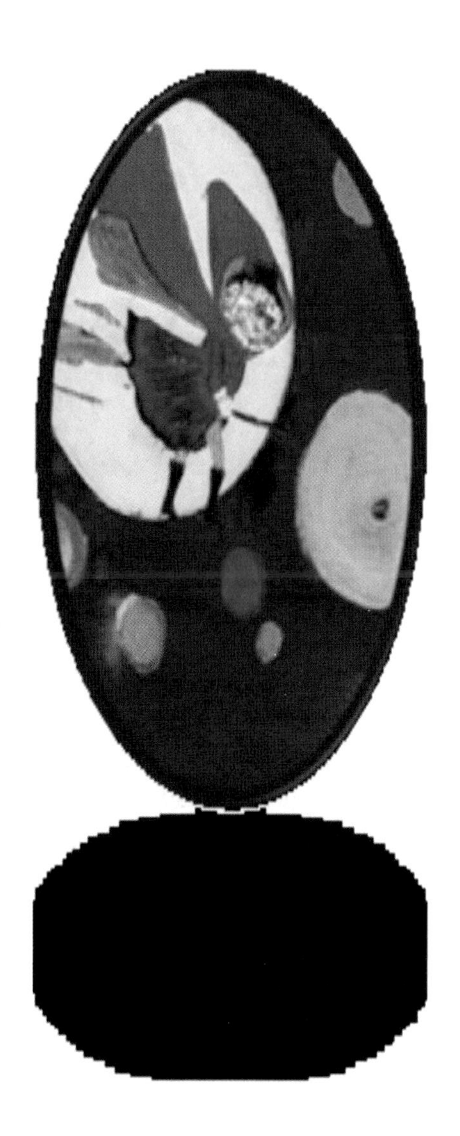

CHAPTER 3
THE QUEENDOM OF NONNALAND

Flying toward us was a lady in a pink cape astride a golden broom. Behind her, sparks flew off the bristles and glimmered in the air. We watched with our mouths hanging open.

She landed in front of Elefantia. Her kind face was encircled by curly white hair, and her eyes twinkled behind her really big round blue-framed glasses. I liked her immediately.

"Welcome to the Queendom of Nonnaland." she said. "I am Befana."

Stepping in front of me, she shook my hand. “Nice to meet you, Andrew, our black-belted math wiz.” She looked over at my sister. “Ahh, our singer, Callista.”

Daniel and Tomas stood side by side. “Wonderful to have cousins to play with,” Befana said and patted their heads.

“Who have we here?” She pointed at Lynda. “You are the girl with the mighty swing.” Turning to Mary, Befana said, “Ah-ha. The curious Mary, who loves animals and runs and leaps like a gazelle.” She stopped in front of JR. He was asleep in his carrier. "Adorable," she whispered and gently touched his head.

Eyes wide, Mary asked, "Who is Cattiva, and why is she stealing all the color?"

Befana took off her glasses, wiped them, and sighed. "Once, all of Nonnaland was a happy place filled with love. We had lots of good foods and wonderful sweets, all homemade, of course. We shared everything and helped each other."

"What happened," I asked.

On January 6th, I was fast asleep after delivering sweets to the good children in Italy. I was awakened by banging and yelling. My sister Cattiva had snuck into my house and was trying to steal my broom." As she spoke, Befana pushed back the hood on her cape.

I stared at her. Something about her was familiar, but I couldn't think what.

Befana continued her story. "The broom bucked and threw Cattiva off. She hit the ceiling and banged her head. That made her angry. She grabbed the broom and slammed it on the floor. I yelled, STOP! Never, ever touch my broom again!"

Befana hugged the golden broom to her chest. "Cattiva screamed at me, 'I am going to burn that broom. Nonna should have left it to me.'"

Turning the broom parallel to the ground, Befana let it go, and it hovered there. She then flipped her cape behind her and sat on the long handle, swinging her legs back and forth.

My eyes were as big as saucers. How did she do that? I scratched my head and walked around her looking for something that held the broom in the air, but there was nothing.

Wide-eyed, Lynda asked, "What happened next?"

"I reminded her of the law," Befana answered. "Only the person who inherits the gold broom can ride it, and our nonna gave it to me."

"What's a nonna?" Tomas asked, looking puzzled.

"A nonna is a grandmother," Befana said, and rubbed Tomas's buzz-cut head.

"Why didn't you throw her out of your house?" Callista asked.

"I didn't have to." Befana sighed. "She ran out, and before she slammed my front door, she said, "'I am going to steal all the color from this land until you give me that broom.'"

Befana pointed to a grey cabin on the far side of the valley. "Look, there. That's Cattiva's cottage in front of Dark Things Mountain. You will see it better when we get closer to the river."

Being practical, I asked, "Can't you give her the broom and get another?"

"No dear. This broom passes from mothers to daughters. Cattiva wasn't in line to get it. She got other things."

"What things?" Lynda asked.

"Cattiva has the power to change things—for good or for bad. And now, out of spite, she is stealing all the color from Nonnaland."

"That's when we went to Sagezza," Elefantia said. "She told us that one day, children who could imagine would find their way here to save Nonnaland."

"And the Neebey birds led you to us," added Befana.

I looked around. "Where are the Neeebey birds?"

"They are hiding in the Neebey Woodland on the far side of Sunrock Mountain." Befana pointed to the bright mountain opposite Dark Things Mountain. "That's the only place they're safe. If Cattiva finds them, she'll send the Cracklors to steal all their colors, too, and they will dry up and fall to the ground like dead leaves.

"No," yelled Mary. "We have to get them back to Grandma's drawer."

"Let's go down there and make that mean old Cattiva stop, so we can get the birds back," Daniel said.

"Good boy." Befana smiled at Daniel.

"How?" I asked.

"By using your gifts," said Befana.

"Huh?" I was confused. Looking for an explanation, the others looked at me. I shrugged my shoulders. I didn't know what she was talking about.

Befana smiled and took my wrist. "You first." She pulled me forward.

"Whoa," I said. "Wait a minute. What are you going to do?" My voice wobbled.

"Bandocker ka drocker," she said and tossed sparkling red dust over my head. When the sparkles cleared, I had a crown on my head and a gold calculator in my hands.

"Callista, you're next. Clio, calo, cleet." She tossed blue, green, and yellow sparkles. Callista appeared in a beautiful rainbow dress that reached just above the tops of her pink and silver sneakers. There was a gold circlet on her thick mane of black hair, and a gold harp in her hands.

"Mary, step up." Befana then mumbled, "Maram, neniram, stythema."

When the pink and purple sparkles that had covered Mary, cleared, we cheered. "Wow!" Mary's dress was a rainbow of purples and yellows, and she had a silver circlet around her blond ponytail.

Befana swiped a stray lock of hair from Daniel's eye, placed her hand on his blond head, and tossed a handful of gold dust over him. "Steady and strong, you are Daniel, the undefeated."

"Me next," Lynda said, tugging on Bafana's dress.

"Teeny-and-tuff." Befana smiled. When the silvery sparkle dust cleared, Lynda was wearing shiny armor and a red cape. She spluttered and wiped the sparkles off her lips. We all giggled. "Our champion," said Befana. "You will fight hard for everyone."

Befana looked around. Tomas was hiding behind Callista.

"Ah-ha. There you are," said Befana, and she dropped a handful of bright sunny sparkles over him. "Tomas, the Knight of Light." Tomas's already beautiful smile dazzled like rays of sunshine, and a glow surrounded him.

"One more." Befana stood over JR's carrier and rubbed her chin, thinking. "Got it! The silent Knight of Milk and Honey." She released white glowing bubbles over the sleeping child. "Look at how he sleeps. He will wake up when it's time."

We laughed and touched each other's new clothes. Then the magic vanished. We were back in our everyday clothes of jeans and tee-shirts, except for Mary, of course. She never wore pants of any kind. She was in a denim skirt with a tee-shirt.

"What happened?" Tomas asked.

"Your gifts are powerful, and until you need them, they must stay hidden."

Befana's smile left her face. "Now, to work," she said. "As you can see, you must cross the river to get to the Neebey Woodlands, but there are no bridges. What will you do?"

I closed my eyes. The feel of the crown grew heavy on my head, and the calculator reappeared in my hand. Taking the pencil and pad I'd stashed in the carrier, alongside JR, I sat on the ground and drew a map of Nonnaland.

My fingers punched numbers on the calculator as I wrote lists of needed materials, math equations, and designs to build the bridge. Everyone gathered around me and stared over my shoulders, even Befana and Elefantia.

Callista plopped down next to me. "What are you muttering?"

"Shhhh." I raised my finger to my lips. "No distractions, please." When I finished, I stood up with my notes. To Elefantia and Befana, I said, "We need to go this way." On the map, I traced the path down the hill along the river to its narrowest point, going toward Sunrock Mountain. "That's where we can build a bridge. The question is, how? It will take too long for us to cut down trees, and we'll need saws, hammers, straps, nails, and screws." I took a breath and scratched my head. "First, I'll have to measure the distance across the river." I looked at my sister. "I'll need help..."

"I'm not cutting down trees," Callista sniffed, her nose in the air.

"We can't..." Mary objected.

"Arguing again!" Elefantia raised her trunk and let out a mighty elephant cry.

We all jumped back in fright. I grabbed JR's carrier and held it close, afraid he'd wake up and be scared, but he slept on.

Behind us, out of the Gold and Silver Forest, a

mass of colors, pinks, reds, and blues swirled from between the trees.

"Welcome, Beryl Beavers," Befana said.

I watched, amazed as the mass separated into individual beavers. "Andrew," said Befana, "they will build your bridge. Show them where."

I walked over to the multi-colored creatures standing together, waiting. They had the largest front teeth I'd ever seen, and their tails were flat and covered with shades of light and dark circles. They chattered to one another, pointing and turning this way and that.

The leader stepped up. Its huge front teeth made me step back.

"I'm Zuppo," said the beaver. "Tell us what you need." I looked at the notes on my pad and told him what to do—beginning with cutting down trees.

Zuppo chattered, making sounds we didn't understand. He pointed, right, then left, then up and down. The beavers nodded then scurried about gnawing through heavy branches. They piled trunks, branches, twigs, and leaves together.

"Next," I said. "We need to clear a path to the water so the beavers can move everything to the shore."

Elefantia called out again, and six golden animals trotted out from the trees. "These are the Galloping Goats. They are exceptionally fast because they each have six legs," said Befana.

Mary hopped up and down. "This is so exciting." Pushing ahead of me, she walked up to the goats. "Nice to meet you," she said. The goats made chewing motions but didn't answer.

I asked, "Can you clear a path for us from the edge of the forest to the river?" I showed them on the map.

The Galloping Goats nodded, bah-hh-ed, then trotted away to make the path; they chewed and ate everything green in their way.

Mary followed them until Elefantia called her back. "You stay with us and don't pout about it."

"Wait," Callista cried out. "What about JR? His carrier is heavy, and it's a long way to the river."

Elefantia raised her trunk and gave another mighty call. From behind the trees came two giant rabbits with the largest, flattest ears I'd ever seen.

"We are the IronEar Bunnies. Like the beavers and the goats, we work together." They hopped to each side of the carrier, and said, "One, two, three," and thrust JR, in his carrier, up, then guided it smoothly onto the flatbed they'd made with their interlocking ears.

"Hooray!" Tomas shouted. We all clapped. The Iron-Ear Bunnies waddled along carrying JR, and off we went in a straight line, following Elefantia. Well, almost straight.

Mary, Callista, and Lynda often stopped to look at the strange rocks and flowers. Giant butterflies in beautiful colors winged their way from flower to flower. The girls laughed and played with them. One butterfly, with black trimmed wings, landed on Mary's hand.

"Oh, wow," Mary whispered, standing still and staring at it.

"Girls, keep up," Elefantia called out.

At the shore where the Beryl Beavers waited, Elefantia pointed her trunk and whispered, "Look. That's Cattiva's cottage."

The shades were drawn, and the door was closed, but the light from inside pushed the walls out, making it fat in the middle.

"It looks like it will burst," Callista said.

Befana hung her head. "Yes. That's all the color Cattiva has stolen from Nonnaland." She pointed to the valley between the mountains.

The leafless branches of the trees hung down, and there were no fruits or flowers or vegetables. Everything looked the same: dull and grey.

"Oh my," Mary said, "It's just too sad."

"Look at the river water," Lynda said. "It's red, and it looks mad."

Out of nowhere, a flock of grey birds swooped down low and whooshed over our heads. We ducked. "Go away," Mary screamed at the screeching birds.

"Cracklors!" Befana said, swinging her arms to wave them off. They are flying back to tell Cattiva we are here."

As soon as Befana spoke, a sound like a freight train filled the air, and a witch with flaming red curls springing out behind her flew to the edge of the river. Hovering on her broom above our heads, she laughed. It was a scary sound.

"So," she howled in a high-pitched voice. "You are the children who will save Nonnaland. Just you try it," she yelled and flew away. The harsh sound of her bone-chilling witch's laugh made us cringe.

CHAPTER 4
RED ANGRY WATERS AND SHARP-TOOTHED DIVING SWANS

Time was short. We had to hurry. The beavers had dragged everything to the edge of the water.

"Beavers," I said. "You've gathered the sticks, twigs, and branches, and I need you to lay them like this," I said, showing them how to build a strong bridge. Like an orchestra conductor, I stood over them, waving my arms to point out directions. Working hard, the beavers grunted, barked, and slapped their tails.

On a gust of wind, a loud flapping filled the sky. We saw a flock of short-necked grey birds with bared, sharp teeth, swoop down at the beavers.

"Help," they cried out.

In a flash, Callista's circlet appeared. Its golden glitter sparkled on her head. She stepped up with her gold harp and played a strange melody. *Ping, ping, pong, pong, pong.* The birds hovered.

In another flash, Mary's silver circlet appeared, and she joined Callista. The diving birds stopped in midair, turned, tumbled, and floated to the music. Stretching their wings out wide, they sailed in every direction.

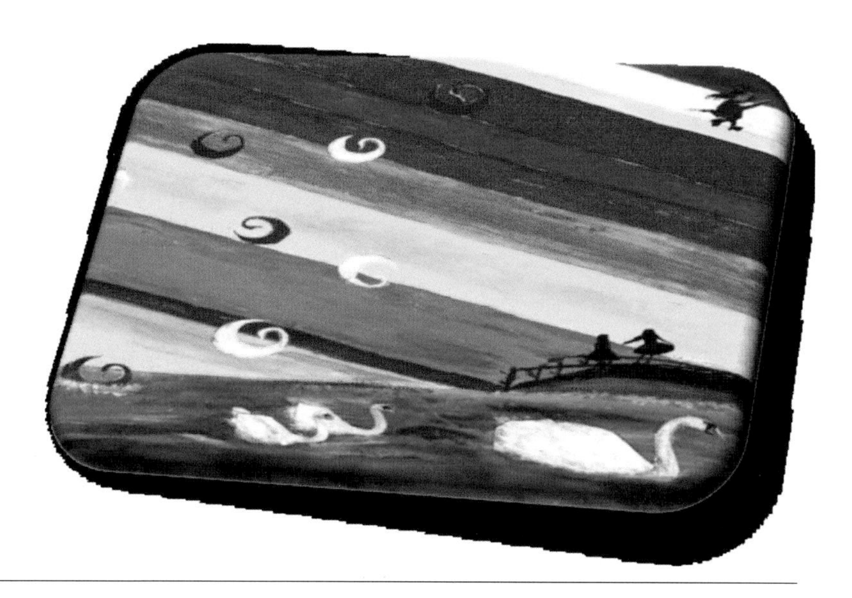

The Beavers finished the bridge, and we walked across as fast as we could. Callista and Mary changed the melody, and the diving birds plunged into the water.

When they came up, they were white swans with long, arched necks. The angry red waters changed to a deep blue, and the swans glided over the surface, waving their wings in a goodbye salute.

Elefantia and our friends from the Gold and Silver Forest didn't cross the bridge.

Overhead, Befana called to us. "This is where we leave you. Remember, you must stay together. Don't let Cattiva trick you into separating, or she will win." She waved goodbye and reminded us. "The Neebey birds are waiting for you around Sunrock Mountain, in the Neebey Forest."

Befana made a quick circle in the air, and landed on the opposite shore. We waved goodbye to her, Elefantia, the beavers, and the goats.

Placing my finger to my lips for quiet, I whispered, "Hold hands." There wasn't a sneeze or a cough as we began our journey around Sunrock Mountain to the Neebey Forest.

CHAPTER 5
MUDBIRDS!!

We walked and walked in the grey land. The air was still. There wasn't a breeze. Nothing moved, and for a while, all was quiet.

Then an alarming sound. We stopped walking.

"What's that?" Lynda whispered.

It grew louder, like a freight train barreling down the tracks.

On a smoking broom, Cattiva swooped in. "I've got you now." She dove, aiming at Daniel. Lynda grabbed him and threw her body over his; we all ducked.

In a flash, Cattiva was gone. The sky was empty.

I took a breath. "Let's go on," I whispered.

Thump! Thump! Splat!

"What's that?" Callista asked.

"Ouch. Owww," Mary cried and pulled something out of her hair. It was a ball of mud. Above our heads waited a bunch of brown, dirty looking birds.

"Mudbirds!" The IronEar Bunnies yelled, "Quick. Take cover." Holding Baby JR, they ran into a cave in the side of the mountain.

An army of dirty birds darkened the sky, flying overhead and throwing mudballs. *Splat, thunk, bang*. The mud balls hit the ground so hard they burst.

"Hurry, everyone," the bunnies yelled, from the mouth of the cave. We ran, but not fast enough. Daniel, Tomas, and Mary were hit. "Ow, ouch!" they cried.

We hurried into the cave. Once inside, we pulled the muck out of our hair and brushed it off our faces and clothes.

Tomas looked out. "They're still there," he whispered.

"How will we get out of here?" Callista wondered.

I looked at Lynda and pointed. "Your armor and red cape have appeared."

Lynda ran her hands down the smooth silver metal covering her chest. Two branches lay on the floor of the cave. One glowed, and one hummed. She looked at them.

"I know what to do," she said. Grabbing the long glowing branch, she flung one leg over it and grabbed the humming stick. "Out of my way," she shouted and rushed from the cave, her red cape flying behind her.

"Throw mud at us, you dirty birds? No, you don't," she shouted and swung the short stick. "Take that," she yelled.

We all watched from the mouth of the cave and cheered her on. Like a powerful hose spraying water, the humming stick sprayed sparkles and covered the Mudbirds. Two of those nasty brown birds grabbed Lynda's cape and pulled her back down to the ground.

"C'mon. Let's help her," Callista yelled. We ran from the cave in spite of the mud still hitting us. We grabbed the creatures and pulled them off her cape. The birds twisted and tried to bite our hands, but Lynda turned and squirted them with extra sparkles.

The birds flew back into the air, and Lynda followed, covering every bird she could see with the sparks.

Feathers flew all around as the birds collided, but when the brown feathers disappeared, their plumage became sleek, black and white, and the mudballs became small bundles of posies. The birds tumbled, turned, and chirped, and when they were all clean, they made a V formation, dipped to one side, following their leader, and waved to us before disappearing behind Sunrock Mountain.

"Good job." We all high-fived Lynda when she returned to the cave.

"Let's go before Cattiva comes back," Callista said.

"And we'll take these," said Lynda, holding the sticks that glowed and hummed, even though her armor and red cape had disappeared.

Holding hands, we filed out of the cave, hurried along the road around Sunrock Mountain, and watched the sky.

CHAPTER 6
BIRDNAPPED

It was a long way around Sunrock Mountain.

"My shoes are tired," Tomas complained.

"I'm hungry," said Daniel.

"Me too," I said. I hadn't thought to ask Befana or Elefantia how long it would take to get to the Neebey Woodland.

"Look! Look," cried Mary. She pointed to baskets of chocolates and strawberries perched on ledges on the side of Sunrock Mountain.

"There's no path. We can't get up there," I said.

"I can," Mary shouted, and took off up the side of the mountain, sure-footed as a Mountain Goat.

"Come back, Mary," we yelled, but too late.

Six Cracklors swooped down. Four grabbed her arms and legs, and two grabbed her hair.

Mary screamed: "Help, help."

I had to save my cousin. I grabbed Lynda's humming stick and flew into the air, muttering calculations, estimating the speed of the Cracklors coming at me, and how fast I was racing toward them.

From behind me, Lynda called out. "Wait for me!" She aimed the glowing stick up and joined me in the air.

"Collision will happen in one minute," I yelled.

Together, we battled the Cracklors, hitting and pushing them, but the birds held Mary.

The noise like a freight train announced Cattiva's arrival. Into the fray, she lunged, her flaming red curls flying wild behind her.

She reached for Mary with her left claw. Lynda flew between the witch and Mary, slapping Cattiva's claw-like hand away.

"Argh," Cattiva yelled. "Drop the brat!"

The Cracklors released Mary, who tumbled down howling, "Help me! Help me!"

I changed direction, rocketed down, caught her and set her on the ground. Looking up, I saw Lynda still battling Cattiva.

"You won't beat me," Cattiva screamed. She pointed her finger, and a burst of hot air blew the glowing stick out from under Lynda.

Both Lynda and the glowing stick dropped down toward the ground. I pointed the humming stick up like a fighter plane and got under my cousin, then turned and headed down to where Callista and Daniel rushed forward with their arms out. They ran, first to the right then to the left to catch the glowing stick before it could crash and break.

"Thank you," Lynda said to me. To Callista and Daniel, she said, "Great save."

We didn't have much time. The Cracklors were preparing to attack again. Lynda took the glowing stick, and together we flew back up and smashed the Cracklors on their beaks.

Cattiva yelled. "I'll get you!" then flew away, followed by her nasty birds.

When it was over, the IronEar Bunnies waddled over with JR sleeping peacefully in his carrier, which rested on their flatbed ears. We all gathered and hugged. Mary was crying and rubbing her head.

"Okay. It's over," I said, giving Mary's shoulders a squeeze. "Daniel, what did Befana say about separating?"

"She said to stay together."

"Yeah," said Tomas. "And she said we have to work together, too."

Sniffling, Mary said. "I'm sorry. I only wanted to get some of those wonderful chocolate strawberries. I'm hungry."

"We all are," said Lynda. "But we must stay together and help each other." Lynda hugged her sister. "They almost got you. I was so scared."

"Me too," Mary said and hugged her sister back.

I sighed. This was hard. I wished we were back in grandma's closet. "Let's go on," I said. "We need to find the Neebey birds. We need to find them fast."

CHAPTER 7
SURPRISE AT HIDDEN RIVER

We were tired after the battle with Cattiva, but no one complained as we walked along the lumpy, bumpy path. "Watch your step," I warned. It was hard to see the holes and rocks on the dark grey road as we walked around Sunrock Mountain. For a few minutes, we forgot about Cattiva and paid attention to where we put our feet.

The land sloped down again. I stopped. In front of us was another river. On the far side of it, standing amid weeds and leafless trees, we saw a big sign with a huge arrow.

SUNROCK MOUNTAIN
NEEBEY WOODLANDS

"Guess that's where we're going," said Callista.

"Uh, Oh," Tomas said. He and Daniel pointed to the water.

Something big and gross looking swam in the murky river. We watched, fascinated.

"Whatever that is, it doesn't look nice," Lynda murmured.

The river beast lifted its head out of the water and turned to look at us. It poked its long tongue out from between yellow and black teeth, licked its lips then sank back down, leaving only its freaky yellow eyes above the dirty water, watching us.

"Oh, no!" Daniel said at the now-familiar sound of a freight train. We looked up as Cattiva whizzed through the sky on her broom, cackling her ugly witch laugh.

"Watch this, my lovely stupids!" Holding a large chunk of meat, she flew over the water.

The river creature leaped high into the air, grabbed the meat chunk, and fell back into the water with a crash, making a huge splash that soaked us with disgusting, greenish, and unclean water. "Ughhh," we yelled and clamped our mouths and eyes shut.

"Ha, ha," Cattiva gloated. "Get across that!" She flew away on her smoking broomstick, howling with laughter.

"Maybe we can turn around," Lynda suggested, but when we looked behind us from the water's edge, a tall, grey, thorny hedge had grown up.

"We can't go back now," cried Mary. Sobbing, she made a circle with Daniel and Tomas. Lynda took JR's carrier from the IronEar Bunnies. "You need a rest," she said to them and placed JR in his carrier at our feet.

Daniel's voice shook as he asked, "How are we going to get across that river?"

Turning to the bunnies, I asked, "IronEar Bunnies, Is there any way for us to get across this river?"

Erble, cherble, berble, the bunnies chatted among themselves.

"Yes. The EagleNuffs can get you across," they said.

"How do we get them here?" I asked.

"You sing. If they like your song, they'll come."

Callista's circlet began to shine. Strumming her harp, she created a song.

"EagleNuffs up in the sky. Loyal friends, help us – please don't let us die."

We watched the sky; it remained empty. "Mary," Callista said. "Please help me sing." Mary stood beside Callista. In beautiful harmony, they sang again.

"Oh, wondrous birds, we need your wings to carry us away. Don't let Cattiva win the day."

Tomas pointed to the sky. "Look!" he shouted.

We raised our eyes and followed Tomas's finger. Soaring on a breeze, never pulling in its wings, a huge bird landed on the path.

"It's an EagleNuff," the bunnies cried out. When it landed, we gathered around. It was the biggest bird we'd ever seen. Preening, the EagleNuff tidied his feathers. "Come now, children, you may pet me. Your song was beautiful," the EagleNuff said. "Why did you call?"

“Mr. EagleNuff," I began. "We need to get across this river, and that awful beast is waiting to eat us. Can you help?"

"Hmmm. Firstly, you may call me, Sir Eagle." The EagleNuff stroked his chin with the tip of one large wing.

"How did you get here?"

Beginning with Mary disobeying our grandmother by opening the dresser drawer, I explained. "We followed the Neebey birds through the magic door in Grandmother's closet because we wanted to get them back before she found out that we'd disobeyed her.”

"Yes," Mary said, hands on her hips. "We didn't even know she had a magic door!"

"Anyway," I continued, not wanting to remind her of who disobeyed. "We met Elefantia and Befana. They told us all about Cattiva and her plan to steal all the color from Nonnaland."

"Yes," said Sir Eagle. "Cattiva is a problem. But for you to reach the Neebey Woodland and save Nonnaland, you must defeat her."

"First, we need to get across this river," I answered, feeling worried. I wondered if we might fail.

"How many EagleNuffs do you need?" Sir Eagle asked, stroking his large beak and pacing back and forth.

"I'll tell you." I took out my gold calculator. "I'm the biggest..." I calculated what we needed, mumbling, and punching numbers. Everyone gathered around to watch me, even Sir Eagle.

"One for each of us, and two for the IronEar Bunnies carrying Baby JR, and his carrier. We need eight. Can you do this?"

Sir Eagle turned, flew into the sky and blew out a funny sound.

"Oh, no. Don't leave us," Lynda cried out, but before we could say *Cattiva,* a flock of EagleNuffs coasted to the ground with their giant wings extended.

"Okay, flyers," Sir Eagle said, "one for each child, and two for the bunnies and the carrier."

In a magic minute, we were in the air on the backs of the EagleNuffs, following Sir Eagle, and flying across Hidden River. The river monster threw itself up, snapping its jaws, trying to catch us, but we were too high.

Once across the murky waters, the EagleNuffs set us down in front of a hill filled with bowls of carrots, celery, spinach, raisins, and yogurt.

"Eat well and rest before you go on your way."

Sir Eagle took me aside and whispered, "Be strong. There are more challenges ahead."

Then, he and his EagleNuffs waved goodbye and flew straight up into the sun.

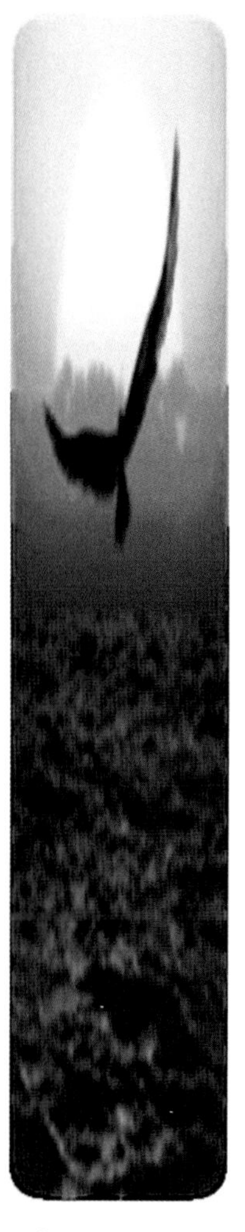

We ate our fill of everything, and spinach never tasted so good. I wished we didn't have to move, but I said, "We'd better get going before Cattiva comes back." I remembered Sir Eagle's warning, and was afraid. What else was going to happen to us?

CHAPTER 8
CIRCLE ROAD AT THE BAT BRIDGE

Feeling better after eating and resting, we followed the signs pointing to the Neebey Woodland. Rounding another side of the mountain, a different problem waited for us. A gully broke the path. There was a bridge over it, but thorn bushes blocked the road to it.

"How will we get past that?" Daniel asked, pointing to the oversized thorns. "They looked as long and sharp as the thorns on Grandma's Prickly Pear Cactus."

"Let's go this way," I said, pointing to the right.

"No," Lynda said. She pointed to a narrow path on the left. "That way."

I was about to argue with her when Mary surprised us. "Lynda and Andrew, remember what Befana said. 'NO FIGHTING.'"

"But I have a bad feeling about this bridge," said Lynda.

Mary took Lynda's hand and mine. "We'll go to the right."

I sighed, happy that Mary had stopped us from arguing. "Let's get a closer look," I said. We held on to one another and walked on the path. There we found a hidden circular road.

"It looks like the only way to the bridge is to take this road. It goes out over the gully then it comes back up and onto the bridge." I traced the path in the air with my finger.

I looked at the frightened faces of my cousins, my sister, and the IronEar Bunnies. Squaring my shoulders and lifting my chin, I pulled everyone in close and said, with more confidence than I felt, "Come on. We can do this."

We started down the road and walked out over the gully.

"I'm kinda scared," Tomas whispered.

"Don't look down. Look straight ahead and we'll be up on the bridge in no time," I told him.

The road circled back up, but it left us at the underside of the bridge, where there was no daylight.

"Oh, no," Daniel whispered. Staring out from under the bridge were hundreds of pairs of bright red eyes.

Bats!

They hung upside down and glared at us.

Tomas, who'd been afraid on the circular path, stepped forward and smiled. A brilliant glow surrounded him, and the bats closed their eyes.

Callista stood behind Tomas. Her gold circlet was on her head. She lifted her arms out and a shiny black cape appeared and spread out like bats' wings. She began to hum a strange tune, singing, "I am the Lady of the Bats. Follow me."

She took the lead walking along the road on the underside of the bridge. She squealed and tweeted at the bats, soothing them. Still aglow, Tomas walked beside her, smiling his dazzling smile, and creating a bright light that made the bats keep their eyes closed.

"Hurry," I whispered. "Be very quiet. Don't make a sound. Don't disturb them."

We tiptoed under the bridge, barely breathing. Callista made her bat sounds; Tomas glimmered and shone. I moved ahead of them to be first out from under the bridge. I feared what awaited us.

And there she was.

In silence, Cattiva sat on her broom ready and waiting. *Whoosssshhhhhhh.* Something prayed from her hand.

My eyes teared. I held back a sneeze. Pepper Spray! I ran back under the bridge. "Hurry," I said. Cover your noses and mouths. Squeeze your eyes almost shut."

I pushed the IronEar Bunnies out from under the bridge with JR in his carrier. Then Lynda and Mary grabbed Daniel and shoved him out into the daylight. Tomas was next. Callista and I were last. We'd almost made it when—

"A-a-a-ch-o-o-o-o." Callista gave an immense sneeze.

In a flash, the bats flew down and grabbed her long black hair.

"Help," she screamed.

"Quick," I yelled. "Grab her." We tugged her arms and legs while the bats yanked her hair, pulling her back under the bridge. Back and forth, we went.

Callista screamed. "Let go of my hair."

Tomas stepped back to the edge of the walkway under the bridge and squeezed his eyes shut. With grunts and groans, he strained and made his dazzling smile the brightest it could be. He directed its fierce glow at the bats. They let go of Callista's hair, and we pulled her out into the daylight, where she rubbed her sore head and cried.

Cattiva sat on her broom, watched, and snarled. "Oh, I'll get you all!" she blew the words out on her foul breath.

Daniel stood up and yelled. "This is the end, you ugly witch."

CHAPTER 9
THE FINAL BATTLE

"Call me ugly? You little pest I'll teach you. Cracklors, come!" Cattiva's attack birds filled the sky that had turned dark and threatening.

Lynda and I grabbed our flying sticks and flew into the air. Mary, Callista, Tomas, and Daniel stayed with the IronEar Bunnies to protect Baby JR.

Cattiva attacked Lynda and almost pushed her off her flying stick. I threw myself against Cattiva and unseated her.

The Cracklors nosedived, attacking everyone on

the ground. They fought hard, hitting the birds with their fists and sticks and stones, while the bunnies covered Baby JR with their iron ears. Only Daniel stood alone, apart from the others.

"Oh, I'll get you now." Cattiva howled, her voice echoing in the sky. She flew up high, turned her broom and dove at Daniel, who stood still as stone on the path.

Everyone screamed, "Daniel. Watch out. Run!"

Lynda and I flew as fast as we could, but we weren't able to block Cattiva as she sped toward Daniel, who remained frozen in place, not moving a muscle.

"Got you now." Cattiva yelled, let go of her broom and reached out.

"Daniel, don't let her grab you," I shrieked, but Daniel didn't move.

"You little pest, I'll eat you for dinner, and my Cracklors will eat the others."

Cattiva lunged and extended the claws at the end of her arms.

Still, Daniel didn't move.

We screamed again. "Daniel, run!"

She was almost on him. Her claws near his face.

Then Daniel raised his arm, and pointed his finger at the evil witch.

Pow! A stream of fiery hot sparkles sprayed out, hitting Cattiva in the face.

The air popped and snapped.

Sparks and flames sizzled, and in a smoky cloud, Cattiva vanished.

As soon as she disappeared, the Cracklors stopped their attacks. They spun, turned, and fell from the sky in patches of feathers.

When they landed, they were doves.

Waving their wings, they took to the air in the direction of the Gold and Silver Forest.

Back on the ground and sweating from the battle, Lynda and I hugged and kissed Daniel; everyone did.

"You scared us so bad. You didn't move, and we were afraid Cattiva was going to get you," I said.

Lynda and Mary hugged their younger brother tight.

Tomas walked up to Daniel and gave him a dazzling smile and high-fived him. "Oh, man," he said, "you were super cool."

The sky turned a bright blue, and Befana appeared overhead, clapping her hands. "You've won! But hurry. Your work isn't done, and time is short."

CHAPTER 10
GATHERING THE NEEBEY BIRDS

We ran along the path, following the signs to the Neebey Woodland and arrived at a thicket of trees covered in bright leaves, but we didn't see the Neebey birds.

"How will we get them back?" Daniel asked.

Once again, my crown felt heavy on my head, but this time, when I looked around, everyone's circlets were shining. Lynda's cape fluttered in the breeze, and Tomas was aglow with light. Only JR slept on, undisturbed in his carrier. We all had the same idea.

Together, we said, "Callista and Mary sing. "Maybe the Neebeys will show themselves."

Dressed in their colorful clothes, wearing their gold and silver circlets, Mary and Callista sang and Callista played her harp. The trees began to rustle. I held Lynda's hand; she reached out for Daniel and Tomas. We stood still, watched, and hoped the Neebey birds would come out.

Lynda pointed to the top of the nearest tree. "Look," she whispered. One Neebey bird had come out from between the leaves and stared down at us with his big yellow eye.

Then another showed itself, then another.

Mary swayed to the music. "Faster," she whispered to Callista, who play and hummed faster and faster. Mary began to turn and whirl like a dervish.

The Neebeys watched her and chirped. Soon, they flew out of the trees and surrounded her. The birds followed wherever she danced.

"Mary, lead the way," I called out.

Mary danced on, Callista played on. We all lined up behind them, and the birds fluttered overhead, as we made our way to the end of the Neebey Woodland, where it met the river.

The Beryl Beavers were there, waiting. They'd built another bridge for us to cross back to the Gold and Silver Forest.

Mary held up her arms and whirled. She stepped on to the bridge; the Neebeys followed, but when they heard an unhappy cry, everyone stopped.

Baby JR was awake and wailing.

The Neebey birds fluttered above Mary's head.

Worried that the birds would get upset and fly back to the Woodland, I ran back to the bunnies to see why Baby JR was crying.

Tomas and Daniel came with me.

CHAPTER 11
DARK THINGS VALLEY

When we reached the IronEar Bunnies and JR, Tomas looked at his baby brother and said, "I know. He's pointing at Dark Things Valley, and he's sad because everything is still dull and grey."

Baby JR, the Knight of Milk and Honey, gave one last cry and threw his bottle as hard and as far as his little arm could. The top flew off, and the bottle shattered on the ground, splattering milk in every direction where the Dark Things Valley began.

Blades of grass sprung out of the ground. Flowers, all different in bright colors, grew up out of the earth. Trees lifted their branches, spreading out like beautiful arms, hands and graceful fingers. They sprouted twigs that ended in new leaves.

Vegetables showed themselves in bright yellows, reds, and greens. JR's honeyed radiance spread up the mountain to the sky, and the sun bathed the hills in light.

Tomas, Daniel, and I laughed with him, patting each other on the back. The IronEar Bunnies held Baby JR up so he could see what he'd done. He gurgled happily.

The Neebeys chirped and neebey-ed above Mary's head.

"C' mon, guys. We need to get the birds back," she reminded us.

CHAPTER 12
THE RETURN

Elefantia and the Nonnaland creatures waited along the road. They clapped and whistled as we passed.

"Thank you," Elefantia called out. She raised her trunk and waved.

Elefantia, the Galloping Goats, Beryl Beavers, and IronEar Bunnies stayed at the edge of the forest and waved.

"Look - There!" Lynda said, pointing to a door that had appeared amid the beautiful flowers and lush green plants. The sign above the door said, *Grandma's Closet.*

Mary danced on, and the Neebey birds followed.

Befana arrived on her golden broom and landed in front of me. "Well done," she said and walked with us to the door. She looked so familiar. Who did she look like? I almost had it when Lynda jumped in front of me.

"Oh, excuse me, Andrew," she said. I didn't mean to push past you, but I want to ask Befana something."

"What is it, Lynda?" Befana asked.

"May we come back again?"

"Maybe, one day. What did you think of your adventure?" she asked.

"We all had, uh, have different powers," Lynda said.

"And when we worked together using our special talents, we beat that evil Cattiva," Daniel added.

"That's right, children. Now, go back through the door to Grandma's Closet and remember all that happened here."

"We shall never forget you," Callista said.

Befana kissed my sister, then each of my cousins. When she came to me, she asked, "Are you too big for Nonna's kisses?"

"I don't think I'll ever be too big for"— I looked into her twinkling eyes.

That was it! The glasses and the hair were different, but she looked like—

Interrupting my thoughts, Befana called out,

"Hurry children. Quick," she ordered, "step across these last gold and silver roots."

Dancing over the roots, Mary opened the door to Grandma's Closet. The Neebey birds followed her in. Callista came next carrying Baby JR, who was asleep again. Daniel, Lynda, and Tomas followed. I was last. Befana smiled at me and winked.

"Hurry," Mary yelled. "I hear footsteps."

We left the Gold and Silver Forest and ran back into Grandma's closet.

Mary opened the dresser drawer, and the Neebey birds flew back into the drawer.

Callista set JR's carrier on the floor and settled Tomas, and Daniel, on their cushions, where they'd been left before we went through the magic door.

Lynda and I shoved the dresses back in place. The footsteps were getting closer.

Catching our breaths, we dropped down on our pillows—and just in time. Grandma walked in with Baby JR's stroller.

"Everyone okay in here?" she asked. "The storm is over, and you can come out."

We smiled in relief. Whew! I thought. We just made it.

"Did you find anything interesting to keep you busy?"

We look at each other, our tongues were frozen. How to answer?

Lynda stood up and gave Grandma her sweetest smile. "You have nice dresses."

Grandma smiled. Her eyes twinkled. "I'm going outside to see if the wind broke anything. I need a scarf." She walked over to the chest of drawers and pulled open the top drawer.

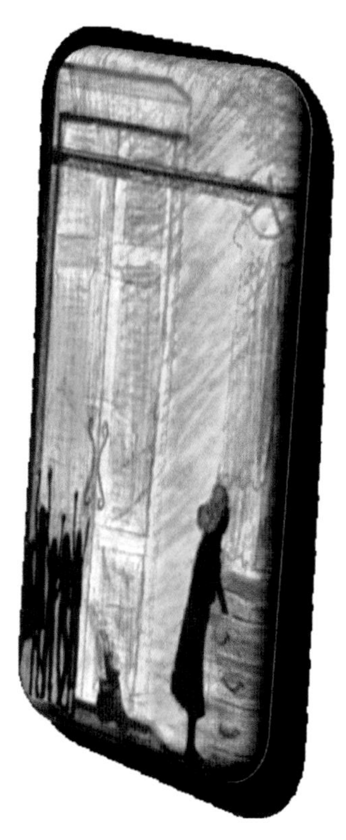

We gasped. Daniel and Tomas covered their eyes.

"Is something wrong?" she asked.

No one answered. Grandma pulled out a bright yellow scarf, closed the drawer, and tied it around her head.

We watched. Our eyes were as big as saucers; our mouths hung open.

She looked at Baby JR sleeping in his carrier. "I see our darling Joseph Robert woke up and drank his bottle." Grandma picked up JR in the carrier, set it in its stroller frame, and walked out of the closet.

As soon as she was gone, we crowded around the

dresser. Lynda opened the top drawer a little; we peeked in. There were scarves in bright reds, yellows, blues, and shiny blacks. I pulled the drawer out. Nothing moved. We started to laugh.

"Scarves!" said Callista. She reached for a bright blue one in front; then, something moved in the corner.

We heard a muffled sound. *Neebey.*

Callista jumped back.

Mary slammed the drawer shut and clutched Lynda's hand.

Callista grabbed me and I grasped Daniel's and Tomas's hands. We charged out of the closet, crashing into each other as we scrambled.

Wait for us, Grandma!" We shouted, together.

Thank you for joining us on our adventure. On behalf of the children and all the characters, especially Befana, Elefantia, and the magical creatures of Nonnaland, we ask that you leave a review on Amazon.com.

ABOUT THE AUTHOR

Ms. Paino has always been a natural-born storyteller and loves encouraging children to flights of imagination. One of her favorite quotes, attributed to Albert Einstein, is "if you want your children to be intelligent, read them fairytales." Whether or not he said it, one thing is certain, and Ms. Paino agrees; a creative imagination is an essential part of the intellect, and fairy tales stimulate the developing mind.

Her first children's story, *Ivan's Double Life,* won first place in California's Foster City Writers' Contest and her first young children's book, *Mama's Little Lady, A Special Pony,* received a Purple Dragonfly award.

In her second children's book, *The Magic Door,* Ms. Paino takes young readers on a journey through their grandmother's closet and into a magical world of strange creatures where they learn valuable lessons of life and togetherness.

A native New Yorker, Ms. Paino, now resides in Austin, Texas, with her husband and her cat, Miss Millie. She loves melding the cultures of her two cities, New York, and Austin.

To find out more about Francine Paino and her books, go to **francinepaino.com.**

Made in the USA
Columbia, SC
21 April 2020